NOMAD'S JOURNAL

NOMAD'S JOURNAL

THE TERRY HENRY WALTON CHRONICLES BOOK 11

CRAIG MARTELLE

MICHAEL ANDERLE

DISRUPTIVE IMAGINATION®

World's Worst Day Ever (WWDE)

WWDE + 20 years – Terry Henry Walton Returns to humanity

Nomad Found

Nomad Redeemed

Nomad Unleashed

WWDE + 23 years – Terry & Char get married in New Boulder

Nomad Supreme

WWDE + 24 years – The move to North Chicago is complete, Kaeden & Kimber join Terry & Char's family

Nomad's Fury

WWDE + 25 years – Cordelia is born

Nomad's Justice

WWDE + 50 years – Terry Henry is taken prisoner

Nomad Avenged

WWDE + 50 years – TH starts his war on the Forsaken

Nomad Mortis

WWDE + 82 years – TH builds the FDG for the final battle

Nomad's Force

WWDE + 150 years – TH prepares to leave Earth behind

Nomad's Galaxy

KEY PLAYERS

Terry Henry Walton (was 45 on the WWDE) – called TH by his friends, wears the rank of Colonel, leads the Force de Guerre (FDG), a military unit that he established on WWDE+20

    Charumati (was 65 on the WWDE) – married to Terry, carries the rank of Major in the FDG

    Kimber (born WWDE+15, enhanced on WWDE+65) – Major in the FDG

- Her husband **Auburn Weathers** (enhanced on WWDE+82) – provides logistics support to the FDG
- Their son, **Kailin** (enhanced on WWDE+93)

    Kaeden (born WWDE+16, enhanced on WWDE+65) – Major in the FDG

- His wife **Marcie Spires** (born on WWDE+22, naturally enhanced) – Colonel in the FDG

1

- Their children Mary Ellen & William, born WWDE+60/61, did not get enhanced

Cory (born WWDE+25, naturally enhanced, gifted with the power to heal)

- Her husband **Ramses** (born WWDE+23, enhanced on WWDE+65) – Major in the FDG
- Their children Sarah (born WWDE+126, naturally enhanced) and Sylvia (born WWDE+127, naturally enhanced)
- **Fu** (born WWDE+28, enhanced on WWDE+75) Married to Gene the Werebear

Vampires

- Akio & Yuko – born long ago, in service to the Queen Bitch

Werewolves born before the WWDE:

- Sue & Timmons
- Shonna & Merrit
- Xandrie & Adams
- Ted (with Felicity, an enhanced human)

Weretigers born before the WWDE:

- Aaron & Yanmei

Werebear born before the WWDE

- Evgeniy, called Gene by his friends

Forsaken

- Joseph (born 300 years before the WWDE)
- Petricia (born WWDE+30)
- Andrew (born WWDE+25)

1775 – John Joseph Dixon

"A good morning to you, Mister Purdie!" Joseph called happily, tamping his pipe as he stood outside the small building where the printing business was located. As usual, John Joseph Dixon was covered head to tie with a wide-brimmed hat, always shielding his face from the sun. He wore the most stylish gloves, because he was an adherent of modern fashion and flaunted his London contacts when packages addressed to him arrived on the latest ship.

"And a fine morning it is, Mister Dixon," Alexander Purdie replied before looking up and down the dusty street in front of his shop.

"We'll be meeting at Charlton's Coffeehouse to discuss important matters, 'round eleven. I trust you'll come." Alexander Purdie was not a large man, but he was of sturdy frame. One of his tasks was to carry bundles of blank print and barrels of ink from carriage to shop. From recorder to journalist to printer to work hand, he did it all. He impressed the ink onto the blank page to share the latest news of the era, news carefully worded to cultivate attitudes and grow the disdain for British rule.

"Charlton's Coffeehouse? Was it only last night I was in Charlton's Tavern? Methinks it is one and the same, kind sir," Joseph jousted. Smile lines wrinkled around Purdie's eyes as he laughed. His cheeks turned brighter red. He was an older man, a widower with grown sons. His printing business had recently been appointed the public printer with the responsibility to print the laws of the Virginia colony. He was proud of that contract, even though his rival Rynd had to die before the honor was bestowed on Purdie.

"You are right, of course," Purdie replied. "A well-educated man interprets what he sees as his reality versus what he is told to believe. Ever since that stamp tax debacle of sixty-seven, coffeehouses have received such bad press."

"Nicely stated, my friend," Joseph replied, using a nail to tamp his tobacco as he dragged hard on his pipe to keep it lit.

To no avail. "Damn. The new crop smells like heaven, but it is not quite ready. Last year's leaf is failing me," Joseph complained, turning his pipe over and tamping it against the heel of his boot to dump the smoldering ash on the ground.

"I don't have anything this morning, but tomorrow I'll need your help, Mister Dixon. Thank you for selling me your share of the business and for your continued help. I haven't been the same since Mary passed. William has come of age, but he doesn't love the work. Not like you or I. Regardless, we are in good places, my friend, are we not?"

"I could not agree more, Mister Purdie. It is best for all. Tomorrow at nine, then?" Joseph asked.

"Eight! We will have much to print." Purdie offered his hand and Joseph took it, shaking warmly, but with far less than his full strength.

Joseph remained on the Duke of Gloucester Street as Purdie returned to his shop.

The hunger burned within. Joseph's secret was dark and tugged at the edges of his mind.

All the time. He fought with it, but knew it would not be long before he had to feed.

Blood was the only answer.

Joseph shivered. There had been quite the stir in Williamsburg the last time he fed on a calf too close to town. Word traveled quickly by way of too many wagging tongues.

Those upstarts who ran Pasteur and Galt apothecary shop knew that the calf's death had not been natural. They didn't believe in witches and searched hard for an alternate answer. While the town's leaders crossed themselves, the apothecaries had rolled up their sleeves and gone to work, studying the facts without making suppositions.

They learned that the calf's blood had been drained, even finding the marks where Joseph's extended canines had found the jugular.

But the leadership was quickly distracted by the churn of events, the inflammatory words of the young rebellion. The speeches and letters of Jefferson, Monroe, Henry, and Lafayette. Two months had passed since Patrick Henry addressed the Second Virginia Convention in Richmond, where they had met because it hadn't been safe in the capital of Williamsburg. Joseph had gone and watched. They'd met in a church and talked, endlessly they talked, but called for action. Patrick Henry was like a caged animal, ready to be released into the wild. He said what he had to say, finally, and then they returned to their communities and their homes.

Henry's words resonated with Joseph and he felt their power. They reflected his own internal struggle. He remembered the speech well…

"They tell us, sir, that we are weak; unable to cope with so formidable an adversary. But when shall we be stronger? Will it be the next week, or the next year? Will it be when we are totally disarmed, and when a British guard shall be stationed in every house? Shall we gather strength by irresolution and inaction? Shall we acquire the means of effectual resistance, by lying supinely on our backs, and hugging the delusive phantom of hope, until our enemies shall have bound us hand and foot? Sir, we are not weak if we make a proper use of those means which the God of nature hath placed in our power. Three millions of people, armed in the holy cause of liberty, and in such a country as that which we possess, are invincible by any force which our enemy can send against us. Besides, sir, we shall not fight our battles alone. There is a just God who presides over the destinies of nations; and who will raise up friends to fight our battles for us. The battle, sir, is not to the strong alone; it is to the vigilant, the active, the brave. Besides, sir, we have no election. If we were base enough to desire it, it is now too late to retire from the contest. There is no retreat but in submission and slavery! Our chains are forged! Their clanking may be heard on the plains of

Boston! The war is inevitable and let it come! I repeat it, sir, let it come.

"It is in vain, sir, to extenuate the matter. Gentlemen may cry, Peace, Peace, but there is no peace. The war is actually begun! The next gale that sweeps from the north will bring to our ears the clash of resounding arms! Our brethren are already in the field! Why stand we here idle? What is it that gentlemen wish? What would they have? Is life so dear, or peace so sweet, as to be purchased at the price of chains and slavery? Forbid it, Almighty God! I know not what course others may take; but as for me, give me liberty or give me death!"

Joseph knew that he would forever be a prisoner within his own body, afraid to die, while being afraid to live. It was his cursed life for him to make the most of.

He chose a direction and followed it, the road out of town, toward the coast. He walked briskly and when out of sight of the townspeople, he started to run, far faster than any human should have. He slowed when he felt them ahead.

British military, coming to join the garrison in Williamsburg.

He dodged off the road, finding a place to hide, and he waited.

When they passed, he saw in their minds that soon they would stop and rest before entering Williamsburg. He followed them, quietly, as the silent predator he had become.

They stopped and sat by the side of the road.

"I need a crap," one of them told his fellows, to their catcalls and laughter. He ventured into the woods, finding a secluded spot to take care of business. He leaned his musket against a tree, hanging his harness from it. He unbuttoned his red jacket, folding it and setting it respectfully on the ground. The soldier undid his trousers and started pulling them down when Joseph struck.

The Forsaken gripped the man's chin and viciously yanked it backward until the neck bones strained, threatening to break. He bit deeply and drank fully while the man flailed, unable to scream.

When Joseph was done, he gagged at the thought of what he'd done, but reveled in the power it gave him. He looked at his victim. A soldier, with his pants around his ankles. The indignity of it and a horrible way to die.

Joseph leaned the man against the tree, pulled some nearby nightshade from the ground and stuffed it in the man's mouth. The apothecaries would not be fooled as they knew what poisoning looked like, but it was the best Joseph had at the moment.

The Forsaken headed deeper into the woods, taking the long way back to town. He wanted to meet with the good people at the so-called coffeehouse.

He could use a fresh cup. Joseph hoped that Thomas Jefferson would be there. The redhead had a way with words that never failed to make Joseph marvel. He enjoyed their spirited discussions.

"Give me liberty or give me death," Joseph told the silence of the woods' darkness. "I shall have neither, but maybe you can, good people of Virginia."

9

IT'S ALL IN THE MISSION – FROM TERRY HENRY WALTON'S PERSONAL JOURNAL

Pre-WWDE

"Why in the hell are you here, Lieutenant?" I asked, irked by his presence. My team had trained together for over six months. We worked as one. We knew what each other thought, their strengths, their weaknesses. I was in charge, but only by virtue of rank. We all had our specialty. Mine just happened to be the equipment. I could tear it down and put it back together again. I made this junk work and I knew how to organize the data we collected and send it back to someone who cared. It was more than a job for us. And I was good at killing people.

I used the equipment for something to do in between the direct-action missions. I liked the scent of a man's fear.

The lieutenant looked hurt.

"Well, Sergeant, I came along to observe and supervise if necessary. I can authorize the movement of this unit to alternate locations without the hassle of requesting it over the radio." The lieutenant seemed satisfied with his answer.

He raised his head slightly so he could look down at me, a weak attempt to assert his authority.

One corporal manned the radio direction finding (RDF) equipment and a lance corporal rolled through frequencies slowly on a radio designed to pick up anything in the VHF spectrum. Both had noticed the friction between myself and the "observer" and watched us closely. A second corporal lay curled up in a ball towards the edge of a rock wall some feet away, sleeping peacefully.

I leaned nearer the lieutenant and in a soft voice, so the others couldn't hear, said, "You stay out of our way. Do you understand? You shouldn't be here and already you've changed our orders three times. I've had it with you. The next time you open your mouth, we're going to pack our trash and we're humping out of here!"

The lieutenant prepared a retort or a threat or something else that didn't matter. I guess my angry glare kept his words from dribbling out like a baby spitting up its breakfast. I'd probably pay later, but for now, the mission would come back online and maybe we could get some intelligence that was worthwhile, then move back behind our lines. A hot meal and a rack in the air-conditioned comfort of our ship waited for us. But for now, we were stuck in a very small two-story building that was heaped with the rubble of a previous explosion.

We had selected this building because it was one of the few whole buildings standing in this part of Beirut. It had access to the roof where our antennas now stood. One antenna was low profile. Another looked like a typical TV antenna, but the third was an obvious Marine green. I had tried to set it up level with the TV-looking antenna, but I couldn't get in touch with the ship. After raising it another six feet, I could hear higher headquarters, and more importantly, they could hear me.

My team was set up on the bottom floor. Only one room was habitable and that just happened to be the kitchen. The only thing that suggested it had once been a kitchen were the sink and the counter. There was no water so we simply set up all our equipment on the counter and in the sink. We had been operating all day now after having been inserted late last night. So far, we hadn't found any exploitable targets and all was mundane and quiet. That probably accounted for some of the friction between the lieutenant and me.

"Hey, TH, it's almost three. You wanna wake up sleeping beauty?" The lance corporal took off his headphones and rubbed at the red creases around his ears. He yawned and stretched.

TH. That was me. They sometimes called me Goldy, too. I had dyed my hair golden blond right before we got on ship. I don't know why I did it, maybe because I thought blonds had more fun. It didn't matter. I guess it was just something to do. Well, anyway, it wouldn't last forever, unlike a tattoo.

"Come on, Stinky, time to rise and shine."

A pair of bright red eyes peered out at me from under the protective covering of an arm. "Oh gawdy, I feel like I just fell asleep," answered a dry voice. He contorted his body into a sitting position and rubbed feeling back into his leg, wincing from the pain of the returning circulation.

I looked at him and laughed silently. Why had I nicknamed him Stinky? Every unit had a Stinky and he just happened to fit the billet. He was renowned aboard ship for his bodily gases. There was nothing he enjoyed more than sharing his gas with others, usually at the most inopportune time. Stinky reached for a Meal, Ready to Eat (MRE) and began to open it.

"Come on, Stinky, you can eat that on watch. Give Plants a break; he's been spinnin' and grinnin' all day." Plants had a degree in botany and went on to learn Arabic. He enlisted because he didn't want the responsibilities of being an officer, nor did he need the pay. He was happy at the bottom of the ladder. "Plants can go suck himself. I gotta wake up."

"Stinky, Stinky. Why do you always have to talk like that?"

"Leave me alone, Goldy. At least my hair's the color God meant it to be."

They never forget, do they? I thought to myself. I smiled and turned away. The corporal on the RDF was laughing as he kicked back on a box turned into a chair. His nickname was simply Jonesy. He never got excited. He was a man who could be counted on, no matter what.

Stinky and Plants changed places. Plants sat for a second, then stood up and began to stretch. Stinky looked at him oddly. "Hey, if you're gonna waste it, I'll take the rack and go back to sleep."

"Nope! It's my turn and I'll spend it however I like." He ended by sticking his tongue out and making international rude gestures in Stinky's direction. Needless to say, Stinky broke into a tirade of cursing. I slapped him on the back and frowned my disapproval, which only served to bring his cursing in my direction. At least he was awake...

It was two in the morning before I finished my report. I had to tally all we had done during the day and send it back to the ship. There wasn't much, but I had to make it sound like we were a four-man army. Only Plants and I were up. I sent the others off to lullaby-land by midnight. No sense in wearing them down when there wasn't anything going on.

I sat up for another hour before I couldn't keep my eyes open anymore. I had been up for twenty-four hours and that was my limit. I had to get some sleep if I wanted to function when the new day came. I woke Jonesy, then quickly curled myself into the warm spot he vacated.

"TH, Terry, wake up! Hey, man, the lieutenant's gone and Plants says he's got something. Come on, get up!" I was dragged to my feet and shook roughly. I thought I'd been asleep for a grand total of thirty seconds.

"What? Who's where?" It was now 0530 and my senses eluded me. I was being shaken and I was standing, but that's all I understood. All of a sudden, the shaking stopped. Far off in my mind, I thought I heard swearing, then a canteen cup of water rained into my face.

That was all I needed, because I balled a fist and prepared to punch at the swearing face in front of me.

"Hey! It's just me. Chill out!" Stinky looked concerned, which was a different expression for him.

"Okay. I'm up. Sorry, Stinky. What's up?" Stinky told me that Plants had been listening in on a conversation for over an hour and that they repeatedly mentioned "hostages." Stinky had gotten up only a few minutes ago and noticed that the lieutenant was gone. He looked around quickly outside the building, but the lieutenant was nowhere near.

"Well, Dick Head can fend for himself. Plants, give me a

rundown and. Jonesy, what kind of line of bearing (LOB) do you have?"

"Just something about the scumbags moving hostages; three, I think, but that's all I'm getting. Those morons can't coordinate what they're doing so they're just swearing at each other."

"Yeah, TH, they stay up on the handset for a long time. Real easy to get a good LOB on 'em. They're shooting a 115 true." I immediately contacted the ship with a short, but clear report. They lost their collective minds and started asking endless, senseless, and unanswerable questions. I cut them off, telling them that I would contact them when I had further information. Over and out. I guess they understood that. About ten minutes later, the terrorists came back on the radio, but this time they gave a firm location where they were headed.

I guess the ship had also been listening in because the radio immediately crackled to life. "Yankee Six Sierra, this is Bravo Niner X-ray, over."

"This is Six Sierra, over," I answered.

"This is Niner X-ray. We LOB your target at 168, over."

"I copy 168. Wait one, over." I drew a straight line from the ship at 168 degrees. Our line of 115 degrees was already drawn from our building. They crossed neatly in the middle of a block held by the Shiite. RDF was not an exact indicator of locations, but it did give a general idea. I brought the map close to Plants and showed him the possible location. He studied it through his John Lennon glasses, then traced a line along a street from my crossed lines to a point only four blocks from where we now sat. "That's where they're going, TH! I know it. Right there!" He

CRAIG MARTELLE & MICHAEL ANDERLE

made a gouge in the map with his fingernail. Sweat beaded on his forehead and his hand shook slightly. It was hot outside, even this early, but not that hot.

I keyed the handset. "Niner X-ray, this is Six Sierra, over."

"This is Niner X-ray. Go ahead, over," the gunnery sergeant's voice came back. The ship knew how important this information was and undoubtedly, everyone who was anyone was jammed into the intelligence spaces, listening in.

"This is Six Sierra. Transfer of hostages currently underway to grid location 4287 3561. How copy, over?"

"This is Niner X-ray. Transmission garbled. Say again your last, over." Before I could answer, mortar rounds crashed into the building across the street, sending stone chips flying in through the window. The entire block was being shelled.

"Niner X-ray, this is Six Sierra, over." My answer was static. "Stinky, get upstairs and check the antenna."

He hesitated for only a second, then ran for the stairs. At that same instant, a cammie clad figure burst through the doorway and slid face first across the floor. The lieutenant had returned.

He rolled over, shock and terror gripping his features. Jonesy shook his head and Plants nervously clenched his fist. I grabbed the lieutenant's collar and pulled him up. I wanted to hit him, but he was senseless already. Not only had he compromised himself, he had compromised our position, and now our whole mission was in jeopardy. I let go of him.

"Hey, Goldy, the Two-Niner-Two is down. The mast is

broken in half and the elements are all bent to hell. The other two antennas are okay, I think. I didn't get too close."

I thought for a minute. The shelling was letting up. Well, at least it was going away from us.

It seemed like we were in the eye of a hurricane, and that's how I felt; we were surrounded by a storm. "Pack it up. We're leaving." My team seemed only too eager to comply.

Despite our haste, it still took over half an hour to load the radios and the two remaining antennas into our packs.

We were set. The lieutenant had regained most of his awareness and was standing, loaded down, just like the rest of us. I had the PRC-77 set up and on, the tape antenna protruding from my pack and the handset clipped to my H-harness. "Okay, stud muffins, here's the deal. Jonesy, you got the lead, then Stinky. I'll baby-sit the LT and, Plants, you bring up the rear."

I laid the map on the counter and showed our route to Jonesy and to Stinky.

"We go fast, understand?" All heads nodded in agreement. "We have to get those eight numbers back to the ship, then it's their ball game." 4287 3561. Those numbers were burned in my mind. I had to get them to someone who could do something with them. The ship had both Snakes (AH-1W Cobra attack helicopters) and Frogs (CH-46 Sea Knight medium lift helicopters). They could get in, grab the hostages, save the day, and get out in a matter of minutes. That was their job.

We had done ours. All that remained was to give them the grid coordinates.

"Rock and roll, Jonesy." He turned and stepped out the

door. Stinky watched him go, waited about ten seconds, then followed. I did the same, the lieutenant beside me. We walked quickly down the side of the street, staying close to the buildings. A couple of houses ahead, Stinky walked at the ready, a thirty-round magazine locked into his M-16. Jonesy was a ways up ahead, looking everywhere, yet moving forward at a fast pace. I turned around. Plants was a couple buildings behind the lieutenant and me. Plants smiled at me, then checked to his rear and gave me the thumbs up.

We had only covered two blocks when automatic weapons opened up in front of us. Jonesy dove into a bomb crater in the street. Stinky broke into a run and dove into the same crater. I stepped through a doorway near me, the lieutenant right behind me. I heard the steady tread of a Marine running and an instant later, Plants barreled head-long through the doorway.

I stuck my head out and gave Stinky the "wait" sign. He waved back "okay." I keyed the handset, knowing my chances of getting through were about zero. Transmitting from inside a building was rarely successful. "Bravo Niner X-ray, this is Yankee Six Sierra, over." I called twice more, then clipped the handset back to my harness. I looked out the doorway once more and waved to Stinky and Jonesy to come over to the building. Jonesy aimed his M16 over the edge of the crater in the direction of the weapons fire. I added a few rounds of my own to cover the repositioning of my point man.

Stinky jumped up and ran straight to the doorway. When he was in, Jonesy popped up and sprinted for us. As he neared the doorway, a machine gun sprayed the face of our building. He dove through the opening and rolled behind the wall.

"Stinky, look for a back door!" I peeked out a nearby window. A number of ragged militia ran from behind a building across the street. Plants and I fired at the running targets, causing them to scatter. Two jumped into the crater Jonesy had just vacated and the other five ducked into the open building directly across from us.

"No-go, TH. This is the only way in or out."

"Don't they make back doors in these places? I'm beginning to severely dislike these people."

"Okay. What can they do? They can call in mortar fire on us. They can blockade us. They can call up some reinforcements. What can we do?" I thought out loud. There didn't seem to be much that was in our favor.

The longer we waited, the worse it would get.

As they say, no time like the present. "Dump your packs. They're staying." We organized our packs into a neat little pile. I took out our one Thermite grenade, pulled the pin, then set it on the packs. We watched as the radios and antennas melted under the extreme heat of the burning thermite.

"TH, something's going on." Plants had been keeping an eye on the building across the street and it seemed that indecision was also gripping our adversary.

"Stinky, you have the best arm. Put one grenade in the crater. Jonesy and I will send a couple more across the street and by the time the smoke clears, we better be around the corner and setting a new team sprint record." The three of us pulled the pins together.

Stinky launched his first, then jumped to the side as

Jonesy and I sent our grenades skittering across the street. The explosions came quickly and we dashed out the doorway. As Stinky and the lieutenant were turning the corner towards freedom, the sound of a rifle crack echoed down the empty street behind us. Then more shots followed. We had been seen.

We stopped behind the corner. I grabbed the lieutenant's harness. "You get these men back to the ship. Do you understand?"

"What are you going to do, Sergeant?" the lieutenant of old demanded.

"I'm gonna distract them. I'll catch up with you, but for now, get those coordinates back to the ship." I leaned around the corner and fired a couple rounds. There was a brief shuffle behind me. I fired another round. Not wanting to look back, I listened as my team moved out.

Then, I was alone. I had the scumbags right where I wanted them. There was no one to slow me down...

JOSEPH RETURNS

WWDE + 25

Joseph woke four years later, refreshed and famished. When he showed up in North Chicago, he discovered the growth and general happiness of the people. They had not welcomed him freely, but they hadn't shunned him either.

He found Terry and Char and the youngster called Cordelia. She had a wolf's ears but also a sparkling personality.

Terry had greeted Joseph like an old friend. "You asked us to have a cow ready for you. We can do that. Load up, Joseph!" They took the dune buggy and with Joseph standing inside the vehicle, hanging onto the roll cage, they headed out, leaving the town and traveling the rough roads of what used to be residential streets.

They continued west for a few miles before Joseph smelled the burgeoning stockyards. When they drove up, Joseph saw the sign—Weathers and Sons Prime Beef.

He smiled to himself. Labels. Even in the world after the fall, they still had labels.

"I suspect that this is the best beef around?" Joseph asked. Terry laughed fully.

"You would suspect right," Terry answered, slowing as the dune buggy bounced over the cattle guard.

An old man working on the side of the road motioned for Terry to stop.

"Hey, Lester! How's it hanging?" Terry called out.

"See, Betty? See? I didn't do nothing and this young whipper-snapper is making trouble!" the old man claimed. He turned back to Terry Henry and gave him the finger. "You can suck my ass, young man!"

Char's purple eyes grew huge and started to glow as she looked at her young daughter. Char climbed from the dune buggy and stalked toward the old man. He raised a shovel as if he was going to hit the tall, beautiful Werewolf.

She ripped the shovel from his hands and threw it away. She grabbed his ear as if he were a small child and dragged him to the dune buggy.

Joseph watched in good humor, not saying anything because he didn't want to be on the receiving end of a Char tirade. He'd already been there, and it hadn't turned out well for him.

"Apologize this instant, Lester, you curmudgeonly old bastard!" She forced his face close to the dune buggy.

"I'm sorry, young miss. I didn't see you there," he stammered.

Cory leaned out of the dune buggy, took his face in both her hands, and kissed him on the forehead. His features melted into a smile.

"I'll make sure nothing like that ever happens again, princess," he said in an old, but tender, voice.

He bowed, nodded to Char, and walked away to retrieve his shovel. Betty was happy that she didn't have to give Lester the big hairy what-for. She hurried to the dune buggy before it drove off and gave Char and Cory hugs.

"Don't mind him," she said, shaking her head and smiling warmly. "Thank you for all you've done for us. It's nice living among people again and not being afraid."

She waved as Terry drove toward the large barn. Joseph was hungry and he could smell the warm blood.

BETTY AND LESTER

Terry laughed lightly, closing his eyes as he remembered when Betty, Lester, and their three cows finally made an appearance.

Terry had been at the Weathers' ranch, when someone started yelling from the other side of the main gate. Terry and Auburn headed out to see who was there.

Once he saw the three cows, he knew who it was. James and Lacy had relayed the story about how Lester had attacked one of the wolves after Ted's pack went after their cows. Lacy had no kind words to say about Lester, but she had thought Betty would be a good addition.

Terry remembered that conversation well. "We can't pick and choose like that," he'd told her. "We have to give everyone a chance. I'm sure the old bastard has a soft spot under that gruff exterior."

Terry had tried to keep it light. Lacy didn't like him and probably never would. It was time for Terry to judge for himself.

"You must be Lester and Betty. I'm Terry Henry Walton, and I am pleased to finally meet you!" he said in his most welcoming tone.

"See, Betty? I told you they was all a pack of shit-eating morons," Lester grumbled.

"Lester, please. Why do you have to be so hurtful?" Terry asked, more in jest than serious, but Betty wanted to answer.

"Because he's just mean!" she blurted. "But there's a kind soul somewhere beneath all that old-age crust he's carrying around. Fuck off, you crotchety old coot!"

Auburn snickered, and Lester glared at the young man. "Why don't you open the gate and let the cows into the pasture with the others. They'll feel more at home among others of their kind," Terry said to Auburn.

He wasn't talking about just the cows.

Betty and Lester helped the Weathers boys stay calm when they thought there was a bad turn of the weather, a weed infestation, or roaming predators. The old people had a good sense of where the young and energetic could best spend their time.

RECOLLECTIONS ON TEACHING GENE TO FIGHT

WWDE + 31

In China, Gene almost died after a fight with a Weretiger.

Since then, Terry had spent a great deal of time turning the wrestler into a fighter, helping him understand how best to use his strengths while limiting his weaknesses.

"As big as that melon is, you'd think there'd be goddamned brain in there!" Terry yelled, spit flying from his face. Gene growled and snarled, but didn't approach. In Werebear form, he circled his opponent.

Terry swung a small club with metal spikes to replicate the claws of a Weretiger. Terry drove the spikes into Gene's shoulder and raked the flesh unmercifully. Gene turned and swept a massive paw through the space where Terry Henry had been.

Terry danced out of the Werebear's reach. Gene attacked again, pulling up short and beginning a dance of his own. Standing on his two back feet, he weaved and bounced.

Gene worked his way back and forth until Terry was cornered. Then the Werebear attacked. Terry counted on his strength to jump over Gene and free himself, but the Werebear was too quick.

A claw swung and embedded itself in Terry's leg, stopping him mid-leap. Gene dragged Terry to his chest, turning the human away from him to expose his neck.

"STOP!" Char bellowed. Gene opened his jaws wide. Char leapt into the air and with the full force of her Werewolf strength, she punched Gene in the side of his furry Werebear head. He instantly dropped Terry and staggered to the side, changing into human form as he fell over.

Terry stumbled, wincing at the damage to his leg. Char gave him a drink of water and together they watched Gene struggle to his feet.

"What happen? I thought I won!" he exclaimed.

"You did win, my large friend. You are getting better with each new day." Terry didn't give false compliments. He meant what he said.

"Next up, a bout with a real Weretiger." Terry turned to Aaron, who looked exasperated. "Yes, you."

"Come on, Terry, he's getting it!" Aaron whined.

"Change. NOW!" Terry demanded. Aaron didn't bother taking his clothes off. He changed into Weretiger form and easily slipped out of his clothes.

The great cat screamed, showing its fangs. The Weretiger focused like a laser on the Werebear, then slowly laid down and started licking its paw.

Terry slapped his forehead. They'd fought together, and Aaron and Gene were friends. Terry never knew what

Aaron would do when he changed into Were form. In this case, the cat didn't seem inclined to fight.

Terry stormed into the sandpit and grabbed Gene by his ears. The big man was naked and there was nothing else that Terry was willing to put his hands on. Gene's face turned red, and Terry let go.

"Show him that a Weretiger cannot better you. Become the Werebear, my large friend," Terry said softly, encouragingly.

Gene changed into the monstrous Werebear. He stood on his back legs and roared, then dropped to the ground, making the sand fly and the earth shake. Aaron jumped to his feet, snarling afresh. Gene charged.

Aaron dashed out of the way, turning and attacking the Werebear's flank, but Gene was ready. He dug in with his front paws and lashed out with a back leg, kicking aside the Weretiger's attack. Bear claws and tiger claws raked each other's legs, before they separated. Aaron circled, limping slightly from his wound.

Gene turned and shambled, but deliberately back and forth, trying to force Aaron into a corner. Char ran to the side once she found that she was between the tiger and the corner that Gene was trying to force him into.

Aaron bunched his legs beneath him, preparing for a mighty leap. Gene surged forward then jumped sideways into the path of the leaping Weretiger. Gene swung a giant paw, connecting with Aaron and sending him flying into a wall. Gene tore the ground up as he headed for the rebounding Weretiger.

Aaron heard him coming and leapt mightily straight up the wall. He kicked against the wall and sailed well over

Gene's head. The Weretiger hit the ground and took off running.

Gene stood as he turned, ready for the Weretiger's attack, but the only thing he saw was Aaron's tail as he disappeared into the nearest stand of trees.

"I'd say that tells you how well you were doing, Gene," Terry declared, as Char nodded.

Gene changed back into human form. He looked around and stated the obvious. "Hungry like bear."

THE BATTLE OF PARIS

WWDE+33

The pods landed in what used to be the Champ de Mars, the groomed gardens standing before the Eiffel Tower, which didn't survive the nuclear exchange between all the major powers. The radioactivity was short-lived because of the air bursts. Many structures had been flattened from the concussive force, but many more survived.

And Paris was making a comeback. They had seemingly endless fields and livestock. France had the opportunity to lead the way in bringing Europe back. They even had limited power.

All of that drew the predators, and not the furry kind. Forsaken and their minions descended on Paris, coming from whatever holes they'd been hiding in since the fall.

Two pods landed and the one platoon from the FDG formed a perimeter. Most of Char's pack was there. Timmons and Shonna remained behind to see to a failed electrical distribution center. Ted remained behind because he always did, but Aaron had come for the sole reason that he'd never been to Paris.

Even though they told him what to expect, he was disappointed when he saw the devastation, when he found that there were no artists on the sidewalks along the Seine.

"What the hell did you eat?" Terry yelled at Gene as they fought to get off the pod.

"What?" Gene tried to act innocent.

Char was covering her face with her shirt, shaking her head as she looked daggers at the Werebear.

Akio strolled off last, seemingly immune to the noxious fumes, although they swore that his straight black hair had started to curl.

"You ride on the outside on the way back!" Terry declared, studying the surroundings. The light banter ceased immediately when the town around them turned silent.

"How many?" Terry asked. Char reached into the etheric and saw scattered people in hiding. No one was a threat.

"Not many. Isn't there supposed to be a mob or something?" Char asked.

Akio pursed his lips and looked around before pointing. "That way," he advised.

Terry didn't hesitate. He waved for Mark's attention and made the axe-chopping-wood motion in the direction that Akio had pointed.

Mark signaled and the platoon reoriented itself into an inverted V. Timmons moved close to the front. Gene removed his clothes, throwing the bundle back into the pod before changing into his Were form. He lumbered to the front, walking alongside Timmons.

Adams stayed near the right flank of the formation, carrying an M14 that he used as a sniper rifle. On the left flank, Private Bennie also carried an M14. They'd discovered the rifles during a raid into old Seattle a few years earlier.

The previous owners no longer had a use for them once Terry and the FDG stopped the two men from terrorizing a growing population. To the victor go the spoils.

Char carried her Glock pistols as always, proud that she hadn't fired them in five years. Terry carried his M4 with the grenade launcher. He preferred the fifty cal, but no one would let him bring that massive beast along.

He was the colonel, but he deferred to the major when his personal bias was on display, although Char never liked the rank. She considered herself a civilian, even though Terry said she was in a lifelong commitment with the FDG. She argued mightily since her life was unreasonably long. She didn't know if she wanted to be in the military in two hundred years, if she made it that far.

She asked him what kind of retirement that would earn her.

"We couldn't afford to pay it, so I guess we both have to serve until they plant us in the ground!" Terry laughed, before returning to the matters at hand. Char held up her arm, calling for a halt. Joseph was standing next to her.

She sensed people in positions that looked like an ambush. He read their thoughts and knew exactly what they planned to do.

"Get down!" Joseph yelled and started to run toward the

right flank. The FDG hit the ground, moments before small arms fire washed over their position. Char and Terry went to the left. Aaron changed instantly into a Weretiger.

The Force returned fire. Joseph directed Adams, picking out the most aggressive targets. The so-called leaders remained behind cover.

Adams called for grenades to flush them out. Once the high explosives rained down on the enemy, it was over quickly.

The Force reformed and pressed forward quickly. Timmons and Gene taking point to prevent further miscues. There hadn't been a single injury among the warriors. Akio was nowhere to be seen. They hadn't realized that he'd gone, but he went ahead to remove the Forsaken from power.

In Char's mind, she replayed how Joseph had saved them. He had been quicker than her and that made all the difference. While Akio had trusted the Force to look after themselves, Joseph stepped up to fill the gap.

TIMMONS AND SUE IN TORONTO

"I thought about how I'd feel if something happened to you, if someone took you, and no one saw anything. I'd want to kill someone, but the enemy wouldn't be there. I see the frustration on Char's face. I'd lose my mind," Timmons whispered.

"We went through that years ago, and you moved mountains for me," Sue purred.

"It wasn't quite all that." He let the words drift away as his mind took him back ten years…

WWDE + 35 years

The pods had landed inside Toronto and the pack separated. They were on a search and destroy mission. Sue had been paired with Adams for the operation and Timmons had been put with Gene.

The Were teams ran into the night, following roads that Terry had pointed out on the approach.

Strongholds dotted the city. The mission was to break

down the barriers between the warring factions, bring them together, and get them working toward being civilized.

"You'd think Canadians would be nicer to each other," Terry joked.

"Maybe these are refugees from south of the border," Timmons replied.

"Touché," Terry conceded. "Cut the head off the snake, if they make you, but it would be best to not kill anyone if we don't have to. There aren't that many."

The teams had nodded and gone their separate ways, figuring they would bring bound captives to a central area to turn loose and whip into shape. People who were happy to be alive were easier to deal with. They hadn't seen any firearms during the reconnaissance. Timmons expected things to go easily.

Only one platoon from the FDG had accompanied them. The Force's mission was to secure and hold the ground once the elite Were teams handled the leadership from each stronghold.

Timmons knew something was wrong when a machine gun barked an angry staccato. He raised his head and listened. It had come from the direction Sue and Adams had gone.

"We do our part, then go help," Gene said matter-of-factly in his heavy Russian accent. They continued to move quickly toward their objective. Timmons remained in the shadows while Gene lumbered straight down the center of the street. As they got close, he removed his clothes, leaving them where he dropped them. He changed into Werebear form and resisted the urge to roar.

They started to run. The target building was unpresuming, but that was where the humans were. Both Timmons and Gene could see them. No firearms. They ran straight toward the front door.

The Werebear broke through it without slowing down. He went left into the main sitting room, and Timmons went right, found the stairs, and headed up.

Timmons could hear Gene slapping the shit out of the people he'd cornered. It took fifteen years, but finally, he didn't just kill everyone he ran across. He limited himself to hurting them badly.

He knew his own strength, but let fly with his massive, flesh-rending claws anyway.

Timmons raced up the stairs, vaulting the last bunch to the top landing. He turned left, then decided to go right. There was the same number of people in each direction, but Timmons was playing a hunch.

He reached for the knob, but someone inside opened it, pulling it away from the Werewolf. Timmons's reactions were quicker, and he jammed his shoulder against the door, slamming it against the soul on the other side.

Timmons jumped over the man as he fell. Two other people in the room smoothly pulled their pistols, but Timmons accelerated to Werewolf speed. He hit the closer of the two with a gut-wrenching punch to the head, then ducked under the second's hastily fired shot. Timmons caught the man's wrist, broke it, and took the pistol away.

He whipped it across the man's face, knocking him down and out.

The man they came for sat at a big desk. There was a

woman who had been sitting on it when Timmons entered. She was cowering behind the man and screaming.

"Shut up," Timmons said, pointing the pistol in the woman's direction. She continued to scream until the seated man backhanded her in the chest.

"You need to come with me because we've had enough of your petty squabbles. We're going to help you idiots to resolve your differences," Timmons told him using the wording that Char had given him.

"I don't think so. You haven't met all my boys yet," the man said in an accent that Timmons couldn't place.

They heard a commotion in the hallway, followed by the thunder of a pistol firing, and then a wild animal's roar that shook the walls.

More commotion and then silence. Timmons realized that he didn't like having his back to the door, so he moved to the side where he could keep an eye on both. The woman watched him intently, keeping the seated man between her and Timmons.

A heavy tread suggested only one being was coming down the hall. They weren't human footsteps. A confused look crossed the man's face. His eyes shot wide as the Werebear appeared in the doorway. The woman started screaming again.

"Dammit, Gene! We just got her calmed down," Timmons complained.

The Werebear sniffed at the men on the floor. Both were unconscious. Gene raised a leg like a dog and peed on them. Even Timmons was disgusted.

At least the woman stopped her infernal screaming, and

the man decided that being somewhere else sounded like a good idea. He stood and looked for an escape.

Gene strolled from the room, growled at something in the hallway, and continued down the steps.

The man resumed his tough-guy pose once the Werebear had gone.

"What the hell do you think you are, a New York City mobster?" Timmons scowled at the pair. "Get your asses in gear and get the fuck out of here!"

Timmons was in no mood to watch the man drag his feet in an attempt to establish his dominance. "Drop it!" Timmons yelled when the man reached for something.

"A pistol will only give you a false sense of hope. Do you know how the talks will go without you? Try not in your favor, dickweed. And you, shut your fucking pie hole before I throw your dumb ass out that window!" Timmons's patience was gone. He forced his way behind the desk, body-slammed the woman into the intransigent mobster, and then kicked the man in the ass to get him to move toward the door.

Timmons took the magazine from the pistol and fired the last round into the ceiling. The woman jumped. "Shut it!" Timmons yelled preemptively. He threw the pistol on the unconscious body. Then remembered there were two, so he took the magazine from the second pistol.

The two captives were standing in the hallway where blood splattered the walls and pooled on the floor. Timmons could tell that two of the men were still alive. Maybe one would survive. Probably none if no one came to their rescue.

"Let's go, you asswipes. You had to make this hard, not

on us, but it's on you, so get going. The only way not to end up like them is to come with us. And you, you fucking screamer. You're not coming with us. I'm not going to put up with any of your shit, so you stay here!" Timmons punctuated his command by throwing her against the wall.

She bounced off and tumbled to the floor, barely missing a pool of blood.

The man tried to grab Timmons, but the Werewolf was ready. He blocked the grab and punched the man in the mouth just hard enough to stagger him. Timmons grabbed a handful of the back of his shirt and propelled him toward the steps.

The man missed the top step and fell, grabbing the railing and twisting as he landed heavily.

"Get up, you piece of shit," Timmons growled. The man finally gave in with a visible hunch of his shoulders. He got up, brushed himself off, and descended the staircase with his head down.

Timmons pushed him out the door, and they headed up the street toward the central area where the enclave leaders were being staged. Timmons pushed the man hard, but he wasn't used to a workout. He was soon panting and gasping for air. Timmons had to slow down.

Gene grew bored and explored homes and buildings along the way. He changed back into human form when they came across his clothes. Timmons kept the man moving forward so he wouldn't see the transformation. He didn't rate to learn about the Weres and the unknown world.

One squad from the Force had set up a small containment area. Two others were already detained. They didn't look anything like the mobster wannabe that Timmons herded into it. He clearly knew the others because he spat in their direction once he was shoved inside.

The other two didn't like him either, since their response was to attack him. Timmons walked away. Sue and Adams had not returned.

He hadn't heard the machine gun in quite some time, but that didn't mean anything. Timmons needed to get out there and find her, make sure she was safe.

"Come on, Gene. We did what we had to do," Timmons told the Werebear with a nod. "Let's go find the others."

"No problem," Gene agreed, watching the scrum within the containment area while he walked away. The warriors sent two men in to break up the fight, while three others kept their weapons raised, ready to end lives if it was a scam.

The eerie silence weighed on Timmons's soul. He started to run, then broke into a sprint. Gene hustled to keep pace, but gave up quickly and opted for his Werebear form, which was much faster than his human version.

The Werebear passed Timmons even though he was running at Were speed. Timmons was amazed as he struggled to keep up.

They could sense Sue and Adams ahead, but they were separate, in too-far different places. Gene broke right to run after Adams. Timmons went left. Sue was underground, and Adams was on the fourth floor of a taller building.

Timmons didn't feel that Sue was in distress, but his anxiety rose like bile into his throat. She was surrounded by humans and small animals. Dogs, maybe rats. He didn't like it one bit.

He ran past a house, then a store, and couldn't find where she was. The basements didn't lead to her. He looked around in panic.

A manhole cover.

The sewers.

He plunged a finger into the space and with his enhanced strength, he ripped the manhole cover off and threw it aside. He looked into the darkness and decided not to bother with the ladder. He jumped to the center of the hole with his hands over his head and dropped through, landing lightly less than fifteen feet down.

He heard them down one of the tunnels. He ran, splashing through the water, making noise to let them know he was coming. Sue already knew. She could feel his presence.

Timmons slowed as he approached a corner, around which light shone. He could hear rough voices up ahead. Young men sounding confident.

"Show us your tits, blondie!"

"I thought Canadians were supposed to have more manners," Sue replied smoothly, not intimidated by the group.

Timmons stopped, leaned around the corner, and saw six men of various ages and rats. Rats were everywhere within the tunnel. It struck the Werewolf as odd how the rats were acting like a trained pack.

"What the fuck is that supposed to mean?" a younger man snarled. It was rare that people called their country by its name. Nothing like that mattered.

Timmons strolled in.

"You brought backup. Good for you," another said flatly. He signaled with his arms, and three of the group separated and rushed toward Timmons. Half the rats came with them.

Timmons hated playing defense.

He attacked with reckless abandon, killing the three men in the span of two heartbeats. He grabbed the legs of one of the dead and started swinging the man around, sweeping the rats before him.

Sue was taking care of business. When Timmons risked a look, two of the men were down, and she had the third by the throat. He had stopped the rats and was holding them in place. Timmons wished he'd thought of that.

He threw the body from him and high-stepped to get behind Sue. The man continued to hold the rats back.

She laughed and it was music to his ears. He leaned in to nibble on her neck. She tilted her head to let him. The man in her grasp looked shocked.

"Take your vermin and leave. Thank your God that we let you live," Sue ordered. The man nodded. She let go, and he ran down the tunnel with a small army of rats running after him.

"That was magnificent, my love," Timmons whispered. "I was so worried when you weren't back with the others..."

He didn't know what else to say. He wasn't the touchy-feely sort, but he'd grown soft in his old age.

Or maybe he'd just gotten smarter. "I'm happy you're okay, because I don't know what I'd do without you," he muttered.

Sue had hugged him fiercely.

Just like he was doing to her now. Timmons came back to himself, back to the present.

She looked at him as his eyes glistened.

"This has been the best twenty-five years of my life," he whispered.

THE DEATH OF GENERAL TSAO

Lieutenant Blackbeard sat next to the young sergeant in the pod as they transited from North Chicago to their next battle. The others in the platoon relaxed. Some slept. They'd be busy soon enough and would need their energy.

Blackie decided that the sergeant needed an education.

"You remember General Tsao?" Blackie asked. The younger man shook his head.

"That fucker had an army when we cut the head off that snake by killing his Forsaken boss, but the general was a total candy-ass, wouldn't meet the colonel to talk about things after their boys lost their heads," Blackie said, nodding and thinking about the limited role the platoon had guarding the entrance to the mine while the colonel, the major, and their chosen few went into the mine.

They hadn't come out the way they went in. Most of them had been limping or dripping blood. But the mission had been accomplished.

Mostly.

"We had some captives, but they got a bit uppity. A

couple got killed, but we let one go with a message. He didn't come back, so we kept the others tied up and we left. Turns out, there was a general down there who told his boys that we were lying scum and that we would kill him if he came up the hill to talk with us." Blackie wiped the sweat from his forehead, wondering why he felt hot. Usually the pods were the perfect temperature, no matter how they were flying, high, low, fast, or slow.

The general and the army remained intact, but without the Forsaken to drive them, the colonel didn't think they'd be a threat. It took five years before General Tsao found his groove.

"Five years later, Akio comes and gets us to deal with this general and his army that was cruising through the countryside demanding that people worship him," Blackie said, grinning.

"I'm thinking that the colonel was less than amused by that," the younger man said.

"He wasn't happy at all, but they had an army. The colonel didn't care. We landed in the middle of the night and set up a sweet ambush between where General Tsao was camped and his next bunch of victims. We set up clay-mores on the sides of the road, heavy machine guns on the hillsides, even dialed up a couple of mortars. Those asswipes only had crossbows, but there was a shitload of them..." Blackie's eyes unfocused as he stared at the jeep in front of him.

"Sergeant Blackbeard," the colonel whispered. Blackie jumped. It was pitch black outside, and he hadn't heard the colonel approach. He hadn't thought he'd been sleeping but checked his eyes with his fingers to make sure they were open.

"They'll arrive before first light, but you'll see them. They're carrying torches and lanterns. Let the first group get past you, there, and then listen for the claymores. When they go off, you need to fire that instant, into their ranks. Sweep the road. Keep your eyes peeled for them to organize and charge your position. Put Bennie into a position to pick off the leaders. Got it?"

"Sir, if you pointed, I couldn't see it. It's pitch black out here!" Blackie replied.

"Sorry about that," Terry said, grabbing Blackie's arm and physically chopping with it in the direction that Terry wanted Blackie and his squad to focus.

"Got it." Blackbeard dug in the dirt ahead of his position to make a trench that he could use to orient himself once it was light enough to see the line of sight past which the enemy would travel. His squad was responsible for everything from that line backward.

The corporal looked to his right, but couldn't see any of his people. He knew they were there because he'd put them in place when the moon was still out and he could see. He stood his rifle up against the edge of the small depression they occupied as a guide for him when he stumbled his way back to his position on the squad's left flank.

He carefully felt his way along the ground until he inadvertently ran into his first warrior.

"Sorry. Sergeant Blackbeard here. That you, Thomas?" he asked. The man confirmed it, and Blackie repeated the guidance he'd gotten from the colonel. He could have told Thomas to pass it on, but then the message would have become convoluted by the last person. Blackie wanted to eliminate any chance of getting the orders wrong.

He continued from one warrior to the next until he reached the right flank. Then he retraced his steps, trying to avoid stepping on his people, but it didn't work. He kicked and stumbled over every member of his squad on his way back to his position. Blackie almost fell on his rifle after one last trip.

"Could you make any more noise?" Thomas whispered harshly.

"Sorry," Blackie mumbled, before settling in to wait. It was still too dark to see. Blackie played with his rifle, diddled with the dirt and rocks, and daydreamed.

A hand grabbed him on the shoulder.

"Dammit!" he exclaimed, and his hand convulsed around his rifle. He always kept his finger off the trigger except when he was ready to fire, for times just like that. The weapon was also on safe, but the best safety was not having a finger on the trigger.

"Shhh," Terry Henry cautioned. "They are coming. I figure it'll be about fifteen minutes before all hell breaks loose. Be ready."

As silently as he arrived, the colonel disappeared into the night.

"Thomas," Blackie said in a low voice. "Enemy inbound. ETA fifteen mikes. Pass it down."

He heard the first couple people pass it from one to the other, then the sound was lost in the darkness as they cupped their hands to keep the sound from traveling beyond where it was intended.

Almost immediately, Blackbeard saw the glow from the

lanterns. They weren't carrying torches as they had expected, only lanterns held on long poles. They walked quickly, as if in a hurry. Maybe they were behind schedule on their world domination efforts.

The corporal snickered. *This ambush is going to put a real crimp in your plans,* he thought.

His thumb rested lightly on the selector lever of his M4 carbine. The squad leaders had illumination rounds loaded and his first shot would light up the kill zone. The squad should already be firing at that point since the action would be initiated by activating the claymore mines.

The claymores were command-activated, which meant that the colonel and a couple of the others were hiding somewhere down there, closer to the road. They'd trigger the device and it would send seven hundred steel balls through a sixty-degree arc to a range of one hundred yards.

General Tsao's army would have no defense against it. Blackie started to feel bad.

He was just like the soldiers hiking along the road below. Follow orders. Trusting that their leader was doing the right thing.

But they'd pillaged and done things that no decent army would do. He clenched his jaw and prepared to fire. They were his enemy and about to learn what real power was all about.

The near simultaneous eruption of five claymore mines was both deafening and blinding. Blackie repeatedly blinked before sending the illumination round skyward. It arced high over the devastated enemy formation, popped, and the parachute deployed. They'd have a couple minutes of near daylight in which to identify and eliminate individual targets.

Blackie's squad started to fire slowly. No one could have anticipated the shock of the claymores. They'd never seen such a demonstration since they were careful about expending munitions during training. Ammunition and explosives were a finite resource.

Once the area was well lit with the first of three rounds, fire increased significantly.

The road below was a mass of the dead and dying. Lucky souls on the far side of the formation, having been shielded by the bodies of their brethren, were running back along the road.

Jim's squad was at the far end to seal off the kill zone. Grenades started to explode in the road before those fleeing.

The general's soldiers who aimed their crossbows into the hills died quickly. Many others threw their hands up in surrender. Some of them were shot, but the warriors reined in their fire when they realized that the enemy was giving up.

Near the front of the formation, single shots from a high-powered rifle sounded with a regular rhythm as Bennie picked off the leadership.

As the flare burned out, the firing had stopped. Someone sent up a second flare, but there were no hostiles left.

Blackie called for his squad to cease fire and prepare to head down the hill. He saw the colonel walking up the road and heard him yelling at the soldiers to kneel and put their hands behind their heads. Aaron was behind him, translating his words into Chinese.

Two soldiers charged the colonel, which was a huge mistake on their part. He caught the end of the spear and tore the weapon from the soldier's hands. Terry used it to block the other man's attack. When he was within arm's reach, he punched one of them in the throat, vaulted over the man as he fell to his knees, and grabbed the second by his head.

A quick twist broke the soldier's neck and Terry let him drop. He continued to walk down the line, ordering those who surrendered to their knees. When he reached the armored carriage in which the general rode, he found the man with a single bullet hole in his head. His closest advisors had died in the same way.

Terry turned to the darkness of the road ahead and gave a hearty two thumbs up to the platoon's sniper, Corporal Bennie.

Blackie returned to the present, where he was sitting in the pod next to Sergeant Nickles. Everyone was listening intently to the story. Some had been there, most had not. It had been twenty years ago that the Force de Guerre had destroyed the army of General Tsao.

"Over a thousand soldiers walked down that road, one hundred seventeen lived to see the sunrise. That's the story people need to know. Get on the wrong side of the new world, and the FDG is coming for you. Fuck those guys," Blackie said without looking at anyone in the pod.

KAEDEN AND MARCIE

WWDE+44

The spring morning sent a misty fog rolling in from the lake. Kae liked to walk along the shore in the morning, a habit he'd picked up from his father. Everything the colonel fought for was so people like Kaeden could enjoy the peace and serenity of the world around them without having to be afraid.

Terry had insulated the people from influences from the outside.

People. What Kae's father meant was civilians, those not serving in the Force de Guerre.

Kaeden knew what his father meant. Many bristled at the term, but they wouldn't say anything to the man who had saved most of their lives by bringing them to North Chicago. And now they had running water and electricity, those things that soon came to be taken for granted. Kae wouldn't forget. It was the FDG that made all things possible. And the FDG was Terry Henry Walton.

Kae thought he could do more good as a member of the

fishing fleet and a defender of all things Terry Henry from outside the FDG. There was an unspoken barrier, even though Kae's father did everything he could to keep the warriors integrated with the community—working the fields, helping in the kitchen, moving, cleaning, and building. Nothing was beneath or beyond them.

And still people bad-mouthed him. Terry sloughed it off. He didn't shoot back. He defended their right to speak their mind. He also defended the right of people who didn't want to listen to mindless drivel. Terry explained about the risks of a free society until he was blue in the face, but there were those who abused it on both sides.

"More control!" some screamed.

"We're free, so why do we need a military?" others claimed. Kae found that he was better distancing himself from the whole conversation and simply leading by example. Enjoying the freedoms earned by the warriors, while living his life to the fullest and not bending a knee to anyone.

A ripple in the water distracted him. Someone swimming. *A little cool,* he thought, but stepped to the water's edge and dipped a finger in. *Too cold!*

He looked at the swimmer, wondering why he would tolerate that instead of going for a run where the weather was perfect. Kae planned to pound out some miles, run to the power plant and back before the fishing boat headed out.

"What are you looking at, perv?" Marcie called. Kae realized he'd been staring, but hadn't been looking at her. Of course, it was Marcie. He saw the blond hair.

Now. She was hard to miss.

"Nothing! I was thinking about dad and the FDG."

"I'm nothing, you say? You're looking at a naked woman and thinking about your dad. I was right. You are a perv." She motioned for him to turn around so she could get out.

He complied without question. When she cleared her throat, he turned around. She had her towel around her, but it didn't cover much.

Kae did a double-take.

"When did we grow up?" he asked softly.

"What do you mean?"

"You look incredible. I mean, it's hard not to see how beautiful you were as we grew up, but I always thought of you as my younger sister. I am not thinking of you like that right now. My god, Marcie! You made my heart skip a beat."

Kae looked uncomfortable while talking. He wasn't one to share what he was feeling. He'd learned that from his father, despite how much his mother tried to break them both from it. Kimber also kept her emotions inside, letting them stew until she exploded. Cory was helping her, even though she was younger than Marcie.

Beautiful Marcie.

"I don't know what to say," Marcie said softly as she moved closer. Kae's breath caught as her towel dropped, seemingly of its own accord. She wrapped her arms around him and rubbed her cheek on his, whispering as her lips brushed Kae's ear.

"A man will chase a woman only until she catches him."

The World According to Clovis

So many people! I love people! the dog thought. *Hear me roar in joy!*

The coonhound puppy barked and barked until he was picked up.

Wow! I sing the song of my people and someone picks me up! Look at that food! I love being picked up!

"Shh, little puppy. Look at those big eyes. Who's a good boy?" said a woman with blue eyes and a silver streak in her otherwise black hair.

Who? I have to know! Who's a good boy? Clovis asked, whimpering, engrossed in anticipation. *Ooh. Have to pee. Ah, all better now. Where were we?*

"Clovis!" the pretty young woman said, holding the puppy at arm's length as she looked at the wet spot on her pants leg.

Wow! Look at that sammich. That little boy has a sammich. Put me down! Clovis thought. Almost in response, he was set gently on the ground. He bolted like greased lightning.

54

At least that was what he thought as he stumbled and tripped his way to the proffered sandwich. With one final superdog leap, he cleared the final blades of grass. His dog mouth wrapped around the sandwich and his terrifying assault ripped the sandwich from the young boy's grip. He started to cry.

Clovis gulped the sandwich down. *Sammich and play! I love people.* An older woman started to chase him and he ran, dodging under a table, among chairs, and between legs until she gave up.

"Shoo, you mangy cur!"

Another dog! Where'd you come from? Clovis growled and snapped, prancing back and forth in challenge to his fellow canine. The wolf bitch raised a paw and smacked the puppy on the head.

Ow! Clovis cried and started to whimper. *What did you do that for?*

Go away, she told him.

I want to be big like you! Clovis said, happy once again, the surprise and pain of being on the wrong end of a wolf's paw long forgotten.

"Clovis!" the pretty young woman called. The dog looked around, but couldn't see her. When he turned back, he had to dodge out of the way as the wolf tried to pee on him.

Hey! Clovis squatted and peed in the same spot, to add his mark to the wolf's stench

"What did you get into?" Clovis looked back to see two hands wrap around his sides and pick him up. Her round human face came close and sniffed. His tongue lashed out and caught her nose. She tickled his nose back. He liked her. Clovis licked her fingers. He tasted jerky. Which reminded him. He was hungry.

Clovis thought the ledge had been lower. He'd always jumped onto it without issue, but it just seemed higher today. "Come on, boy," the tall and dark-skinned man called. He was heading to the barn where he kept some of the cows. It used to be fun chasing the cows, but then the human...all the yelling...it was still worth it. After getting kicked, Clovis decided that maybe his humans were right.

He panted as he loped after the man. It was just them while the others were gone. Did they leave yesterday? Maybe months ago? Clovis couldn't remember. The females had their work and the males had their manly work. Clovis chose the manly work, in the pasture with the cows.

Auburn looked at Clovis's graying face. "We need to build you a ramp, don't we, old boy?" he asked. Clovis cocked his head one way, and then the other. He wasn't sure what the man was saying, but he talked all the time. Clovis listened because it was his job. The female had said so.

The barn was packed with cattle. Auburn moved them to clear the way so he could get past. Clovis stayed on his heels.

"It's about time, isn't it, girl?" he asked the cow struggling with labor. Crimson was there, Alabama's boy. He had been there all along and whistled as she got close.

Auburn wanted to be there at the birth, just in case. Crimson was still training. He hadn't seen it all yet.

Clovis stared at the process. He stood, mouth slack, as he watched. He'd seen it before, but it always amazed him how cows could poop out baby cows. Clovis always looked and sniffed at his butt, wondering why he never produced a puppy. He figured that he wasn't eating the right stuff.

Auburn was relaxed and calm, which made Clovis calm. The calf was born without issues and the big man cleared the way so they could leave. He didn't go to the house, though, but the stable, where he hitched the horse to their cart. He waved for Clovis to jump in, but it was too high.

Clovis whimpered. *I'll just run alongside, if that's okay,* he thought.

"You ride up here with me!" the nice man said, getting down to pick Clovis up and put him up front.

I can see the whole world from up here! he exclaimed as he sat on the padded bench next to the human. The ride was fraught with danger and adventure as Clovis imagined crazed beasts attacking from all sides. He barked at them as the man rubbed his back and held him close.

The cart rolled into the main community of North Chicago and Clovis's favorite spot, the park where there were always other dogs and people. Children, mostly. He loved the children.

When the cart stopped, Clovis leaned over the edge to jump down.

"Hang on, boy," the man said kindly. He got down first and walked around to where he could get a good grip and lower the old coonhound to the ground. Clovis wagged his tail furiously. He loped away, looking for something to eat, but he heard a voice.

The musical voice of the one with glowing blue eyes. He hoped she had some jerky. She did last time he saw her. Was that yesterday? It didn't matter, even yesterday was forever long ago.

He saw her! There with the others. His whole pack. Holy crap! He ran toward them, reveling in his speed. He leapt for her. A big man stepped in the way and caught Clovis. "Hey, buddy!" Terry said, holding Clovis close.

Terry leaned close to Cordelia so Clovis could lick her face. "When are you going to train this dog?"

GENE AND FU'S EPIC JOURNEY TO THE CRIMEA

Gene and Fu left Petersburg with a huge bag of food and household items that Gene carried nonchalantly over one shoulder. It weighed twice as much as Fu, but he didn't care. They were going someplace warm, because Fu was cold in Petersburg.

The Werebear didn't even question the journey. Once Fu said she couldn't get warm, the decision made itself.

Gene wasn't sure how to get there.

"Where is Crimea?" Fu asked innocently as they walked. Even though Gene shortened his stride, Fu still skipped and hopped every third step to keep pace.

"Head south. Hit Black Sea. Turn left, find Crimea," Gene replied.

She looked at him out the corner of her eye.

"I don't know," the big man admitted.

Fu smiled and giggled.

"I think it will be okay," she suggested.

"Of course!" the big man bellowed in his heavy Russian

accent. "We are together, Evgeniy and Fu, Fu and Evgeniy, as it shall always be."

Fu smiled and tried to adjust her hand. She could only see her wrist. Gene's fingers could wrap around her hand twice, but at least it was warm. Gene was always warm.

Her personal bear rug. She'd been a servant, but no more. Gene saved her from that life. Sometimes she wondered how she deserved the adoration of such a man, but stopped when she realized that those thoughts wasted time. She accepted it, without taking it for granted.

Gene needed so very little from her. He only wanted to love her. The big man, older than she would ever know, had never been in love. The sparkle in Fu's almond-shaped, big brown eyes drew him to her, made him feel different, self-conscious.

He worried that he was too big, too gruff for such a delicate flower.

She worried that she was too fragile for a man with strength like his. He picked her up and carried her like a child, but she never felt childish. And he was gentle.

"Why you love me, Gene?" she asked in her lilting accent.

"Because you are my Fu," he answered simply, unsure of the question.

"Gene," Fu said, prodding him in the chest with her tiny finger as she relaxed in his arm with her head on his shoulder.

"You make me feel..." Gene started slowly, looking down at the ground as he plodded forward, step after step. "I feel everything better, colors are brighter, air is cleaner, birds sing louder, world is better place with Fu in it."

"I like being in your world, too. You make me feel safe. I never felt safe before I met you." Fu looked away and pointed to the ground.

He put her down, adjusted the bag over his shoulder, and they kept walking.

South. Always south.

The heat came whenever they walked away from the river, bearing down on them. Gene gave Fu all the water, even though his need was greater than hers. And then they ran out, somewhere northwest of Moscow as they were trying to skirt the city, looking for a series of lakes. Ruzos, Gene thought they were called.

Fu collapsed. Gene's head swirled. He yelled at the sky and screamed at the hard, dead earth. He changed into Werebear form and struggled against the greatest enemy he'd ever faced. His love was dying and there wasn't anything he could do about it.

He moved her about with his massive snout until he could drape her over his neck. He grabbed their bag, light because there was no food or water within.

Gene started to lope, on three legs as he held his unconscious wife in place with one paw, taking care not to dig his claws in. Being in Werebear form cleared his head enough to use his heightened senses. Water. He could smell it.

He turned in that direction and ran as fast as he dared, Fu bouncing on his neck and shoulders. He knew that she would be bruised and sore, but water was life!

Gene saw the green of vegetation, hiding within a dip, a valley through which a stream flowed and where a small lake had formed. Gene slowed to negotiate a bank, jump across a ravine, and plowed into the clear water without hesitation. Fu fell from his neck and sank below the surface.

A human Gene swam below her and brought her up for air. He faced her head down and slapped her back, driving the water from her lungs.

She sputtered as he nestled her into the relative cool of the small lake. Gene dipped his face in and drank. Fu's eyes fluttered as she came back to the present.

"Drink, my lover, drink. Good water," Gene said roughly, his hair matted to his head from the road dirt.

Fu sipped at first, then drank more. They relaxed in the water. Gene held his hairy arm over her head to block the sun. Her delicate, porcelain features brightening from their trek under a harsh sun.

They waded ashore where a naked Gene built a small lean-to using the bag, its contents dumped on the ground. He returned to the lake with the flasks, filling them all, while drinking fully in quantities that only a Werebear could hold.

"I don't mind, but where are your clothes?" Fu finally asked. Once Gene's head was clear, he knew that he would have to backtrack a few miles to find where he'd changed form. The three-legged tracks through the Fallen Lands would be easy to follow.

"That way," Gene said, pointing. "I get them and come back soon." He leaned down to kiss her, and she wrapped her arms around his neck and pulled herself to him.

"Don't leave me," she whispered. He nodded and lay down next to her, handing her a flask so she could keep drinking. Caressing her hair with a meaty hand, he didn't remember falling asleep.

When they woke, it was early morning. Dawn's approach lightened the eastern sky. Gene and Fu drank and then bathed in the lake. They moved upstream to drink some more. Gene picked up Fu and carried her in his arms as he ran through the darkness on his way to recover his clothes, his Were-enhanced vision helping him see the way.

It took less than thirty minutes to run the five miles to where his clothes had been abandoned.

He dressed and bowed for Fu as if they were on parade. She clapped before he picked her up and ran back to their camp. Gene didn't see an elevation from which they could learn where they were, but it didn't matter. The sun rose in the east, which meant that the small river leading from the lake was heading south.

They packed their stuff and headed out. There had been no fish, but there were tracks in the muddy shore. Gene thought they were from a deer, but they could have been a wild boar. He trusted their scent more than their tracks, but they were old.

The first day of their new lives was spent hungry, but at least they had an unlimited supply of water.

Gene didn't risk crossing the open Wastelands again. He stayed near the river, following its meandering track.

South. Always south.

The third day and Fu's ribs were growing more pronounced against her skin. Gene knew they had to find food. He was starving, but he knew that Fu would eat first.

Terry Henry always ate last and finally Gene understood why. Everyone needed somebody to take care of them. Terry's love was for all mankind, for the humanity he fought to save. He had taken on the responsibility of bringing back civilization. That meant sacrifice. That meant eating last.

Gene was a Werebear, a solitary creature who fought to live, not to take care of someone else. That was, until he met Fu.

Sacrifice for others, even something so simple as eating last. It made sense. If one provided enough, then everyone ate well. If there wasn't enough, then the leader failed.

There wasn't enough. Gene was failing Fu, but she hadn't complained. She trudged along, smiling when Gene looked at her. When they found the tracks, Gene set up a camp and moved downwind so that his prey wouldn't smell him.

He wanted to change into Werebear form, but there was always a risk that the animal would take over. Once that happened, the human Gene would be gone forever. He couldn't leave Fu out there, so he stayed in human form and picked up two rocks to brain an unsuspecting animal.

Gene counted on his unnatural strength to give him the edge. He tracked the animals, looking for where they found shelter. Roe deer. Not much bigger than a dog. A small family.

Survival of the fittest. Gene didn't hesitate. With one throw, he took out two of them, and the second rock nearly took the head off the third animal. He hurried into the glade, snapping their necks, frowning with the act. There wasn't enough for both of them, but Fu could eat well for a week.

And so she would. Gene ate the minimum he could to maintain enough strength until he found a better source of food.

Fu sensed the Werebear's unhappiness as he cleaned and cooked the small animals. She ate in silence, knowing that she had to, knowing that he had done what he had to for her.

"We will survive, my Gene," she finally said. "I want you to know that I'm not cold anymore."

Gene looked at her and with tears in his eyes, he started to laugh. He stood and started to dance, Russian style, but without music, his arms crossed as he dipped and kicked his legs out, yelling 'Ha' with each movement.

After two more weeks of traveling down the river, they stood on the shore of the Black Sea. Gene had speared fish and a great wild boar that sustained them. Fu found root vegetables and edible greens.

It took both of them to sustain each other. Gene understood the harmony of their partnership. What he would do for her, she would do for him, and together, they were far stronger than they could ever be alone.

Gene picked Fu up and swung her around in a circle. "I already like it here," he told her in his heavy Russian accent.

"Khorosho, i ya tozhe," she replied in Russian. *Good, and me, too.*

WWDE + 150

I'm sitting here cooling my heels while Akio is searching for Michael, joining him to clear the riff-raff from the Earth, something that I was supposed to be doing. Then again, from what I heard of Denver, he's conducting more of a scorched earth kind of thing. I'm not sure I could ever get that far.

But the Dark Messiah can. It's been so long, but we have such good people. I think they hold me up as much as I hold them.

We heard from Sarah Jennifer. She met Michael Nacht. I'm glad I hadn't heard that until later. She survived the encounter and even earned his respect. I could not be more proud. She said she's also getting married.

I'm not sure how I feel about that. It turned out well for Cordelia. Ramses is a good guy, but he didn't mourn the loss of his parents as I expected. In fact, he never said a word, not at the funeral or afterwards. I need to talk to

Cory about that, see if there is anything I can do. He got lost in the shuffle.

Do for others as you wish they'd do unto you, or something like that.

Kaeden and Marcie are still torn at the loss of Mary Ellen. William is not doing well either. It rips my heart to see them crushed as they are. It is the tragedy of life as seen through our eyes, the eyes of the seemingly immortal. Mary Ellen and William refused to go into the pod doc and get nanocytes. They wanted to live a natural life.

I respect their decision, but I don't have to be happy about it. Kae and Marcie have carried me over the years, giving me reasons to keep trying to do better. Char and I both. We could not be more proud of our kids. I need to tell them that more often.

I get caught up in stuff, focused on the next mission. In the past one hundred and fifty years, I have learned some patience. I won't tell Char this, but I can't wait. We're going to space!

I never dreamed of being an astronaut. I like keeping my feet on the ground, but the complexities of space combat! I have zero knowledge of that stuff because there is nothing written on Earth that is based on actual experience. I can't wait! Huzzah!

Shhh. Don't tell Char.

I've been making the rounds since I'm here and not in space...

Kailin is the apple of his mother's eye. Kimber and Auburn are happy that he was boosted. They won't have to watch him grow old. Sylvia came by her nanocytes naturally and is helping Kailin with Walton Industries.

It's kind of embarrassing that they called it what they did. Sure, I have an ego, but I'd also like to think that I'm more humble than that. At least it isn't painted on the sides of the dirigibles in letters fifty feet high.

Ted and Felicity seem to like their new life as patrons of sky travel. They move about the country in luxury with servants and local goods, banquets and parties. Had I lived back then—I'm old, but not that old!—it would remind me of the Great Gatsby era. I would have never thought that Ted would like it, but his engines are making things happen.

I wonder when they'll go to Europe? Things are still a little hot out that way. Michael is there, somewhere. Just follow the trail of destruction. I wonder if I'll get to meet him?

I'd also love to see those pistols he's carrying. Jean Dukes specials? Adjustable power with five thousand rounds? Sumbitch! I gotta get me some of that!

If he lets me. I wonder what one of those would do to a spaceship? Vacuum has a way of leveling the playing field. All you have to do is make a hole and let space take care of the squishy things inside the ship.

I can't wait to go to space! Shit, sorry. Don't tell Char.

Where was I? Sylvia. I think she's going to go her own way. She is a free spirit. Maybe she'll steal that young man from Portland. Not so young anymore, but the pod doc seems to be back up to speed, although Akio and Yuko aren't in Japan right now. They are looking for Michael. I expect they'll find him soon.

I don't know if Magnus Tolliver would consider getting boosted or not. I'd support it, if that's what Sylvia wanted.

All my children and grandchildren are precious to me. I would do anything for them.

Except their dishes. Where did we go wrong in that we raised kids who will do anything to save the world, but they're slobs? How could I raise a slob? I'm not. Char's not, although she does leave her clothes laying around. I can't complain about that. The hottest woman on the whole planet is in love with me and is perfectly happy to walk around our home naked.

Baseball. Ice Water. Cricket.

I miss Gene. He acted like a goof sometimes, most of the time, but damn, he was such a good guy. We tore him away from his life alone, forced a solitary creature into being a member of the pack. He was always an outsider until Fu came along.

Fu! She saved him. Thank God she got boosted. And then those kids of theirs. Anastasia is cute as a button, but her strength is in her community of spirit. She and her mother are bringing peace to a violent world. Gene and Bogdan are pacifying all of the Crimea. From the name, one would think that crime would run rampant, but not with Gene and his family there.

Criminals be warned. Your days are numbered. Here's to you, my massive Werebear friend! I'd love to clink a glass of beer with you, but you don't appreciate it like I do. You have a tendency to chug it and then make a face.

Water for you. I know you don't want to go to space with us. Hold the fort for when we get back. Do the best you can, and we will see you again.

Aaron and Yanmei are more open to going. I hope they decide to come. They help bring peace to Char and me.

Just like Cory. How did we get blessed with people who are so well grounded?

And there's nothing like sparring with a kung fu Weretiger! They got skillz!

I like that Kurtz guy. He's solid. Reminds me of Boris. I miss those guys, all of them, but it is the torment of the immortals. Be careful what you ask for, you may get it.

I don't want to die! And Mother Earth replies, "Okay, but you'll have to watch everyone else die instead."

I digress again. You can see what's on my mind. I think Sue, Timmons, Shonna, and Merrit are ready to go. I wonder about Ted. He would love the challenges of interstellar engineering. What would Felicity do trapped on a spaceship?

That will be an interesting conversation.

There's no way I'm asking those two vixens, Annika and Meta. They are plying the bars as the most popular dancers in all San Francisco. I think they're trying to single-handedly take on the entire male population of San Francisco. I heard Werewolves had voracious appetites, but these two are wild.

I'm not sure who else to ask to go. Cory and Ramses aren't sure, but the other kids are. Kim, Kae, Marcie, and Auburn refuse to be left behind. Auburn is in for a shock, I think.

No beef in space.

That sucks for me, too, and Char. I hope they have beer. Or at least cookies. How to make space travel suck most heinously—no cookies. Or beer. Or steak. What are we going to eat? Rehydrated food packs? Soylent Green?

I guess it doesn't matter. We'll eat whatever they offer us, because, SPACE!

I can't wait.

Don't tell Char.

WWDE + 150, San Francisco

Terry and Char stood on a Treasure Island shore, looking out on the bay. Ships were in various stages of coming and going. The engine droning did not detract from the peace of the scene.

"Civilization," Terry said.

"Humanity has found its purpose again," Char added.

"Yes. Beyond survival. That Maslow guy was pretty smart. Once the basic needs are taken care of, people can focus on other things. But there's still a lot of scratching in the dirt to survive out there."

Char shrugged. The beachhead of civilization would expand outward, giving people more and more purpose. Like history had taught them, people would flock to the cities for a taste of the good life, until that good life was shared in the country, then people would emigrate from the congestion and the turmoil of the big city.

The farms were king, but they were close to the cities.

They would be pushed out, farther away, as they had been before. Not yet, but someday.

Terry and Char held hands, accepting the silence of the moment, drinking in the Earthly air. They weren't sure when, but they'd soon board a ship, take it to the Annex Gate, and fly to another galaxy. They hoped to meet Bethany Anne, the Empress of the Federation. She would be busy, as empresses tended to be, but TH could always hope. Char was more reserved. She wasn't sure about meeting the Queen Bitch herself. Char had been the alpha bitch for over a century.

She was afraid of getting on BA's wrong side with an errant thought. If Akio was there, he could vouch for her. She remembered her first exchange with the Queen's Bitch.

That could have gone better. Terry had done everything except grovel at Akio's feet.

She chuckled to herself. Terry looked at her, then returned to watching the small waves slap gently at the shore.

They both heard the sound of approaching footsteps. They were measured, but light. Terry didn't need to turn around and look. He'd heard them before. Char sensed the etheric energy within them.

"Joseph. Petricia. Thanks for joining us," Terry said. The Forsaken nodded, holding hands and watching the bay.

"Have you guys gone crabbing recently?" Terry asked, finally turning to face his friends.

Petricia rolled her eyes.

"Not yet," Joseph replied. She cocked her head and looked at him. "We may not."

Char coughed to hide her laugh.

"I never took you for one to …" Terry fought valiantly to find the right word. Three pairs of eyes watched him intently. Char and Petricia's looks became glares. Joseph started shaking his head. "Dammit! You never really liked crabbing, did you?"

"I have to admit that I did at first, then I didn't, then I did again. It was nice being successful at something like that. And it wasn't just me. Andrew was a natural. His joy at doing it was infectious. You're right. It wouldn't be the same going out now."

Terry bit his lip, upset with himself for bringing it up. To Joseph, it had been only a few weeks since he last saw Andrew. To TH, it had been sixteen years since the Forsaken had died.

"We mourned a long time," Terry started. "For Andrew, for Destiny Chase, for all those we lost. We're finally in a position to move on. I will tell you this again, but I could not be happier that we finally found you. Alive."

"Us, too. I'm all about being alive," Joseph said, trying to keep it light, but his face darkened with his mood as he thought about his friend Andrew.

"Enough of this. It's time to celebrate the next step in our journey. When Bethany Anne returns with her fleet, we're going to board one of the ships, the FDG, both the tac teams and some of the regular warriors. I would you like you two to come with us to the stars, my friend."

Joseph and Petricia looked at each other. She wasn't sure. Too much had happened in too short a time. Joseph took a deep breath, closed his eyes, and appreciated the moment.

When he opened his eyes again, he looked calm.

"The world descends into an age of madness," he began in a voice free of doubt. "And an age of expansion. Like the wild west of the eighteen hundreds, people race into the great unknown of the new cities, the Wasteland, to find their fortune. Alas, Earth holds no allure for one such as I, trapped between the good and the evil that is mankind."

Joseph pulled Petricia close and hugged her tightly. His wide-brimmed hat blocked his face. Terry and Char watched as his tears splashed on the black leather covering Petricia's shoulder. She sobbed in his arms, briefly, before stepping back, wiping her eyes with a delicate finger, and smiling at her husband.

She nodded.

"Sometimes, one must grieve in their own way. I wish I had a beer to share with you, so we could toast appropriately."

"As do I. It's never too early for beer, is it, Joseph?"

Char shook her head.

"We want you to come with us. Help us with whatever lies ahead," Char added.

"Sounds good," Petricia said.

"You heard the woman. Reserve us a window seat on the express train to the stars."

Joseph offered his hand. Terry grabbed it and yanked Joseph into a one-armed man-hug.

"I am ready to go, my man. Right now!" Terry exclaimed.

"Hang on…" Char started to say before slapping Terry's shoulder. He laughed, picked her up, and danced on the shore.

"Where you go, we will follow," Joseph whispered.

AUTHOR NOTES - CRAIG MARTELLE

AUGUST 27, 2017

Thank you for reading this small piece of Terry Henry Walton history

We had to skip bits of time here and there throughout the storyline in order to keep things moving forward. We were severely limited by the ten books (okay, that was a self-imposed limitation), so we had to cover 150 years!

The series was still ¾ of a million words strong.

And we still needed these short stories to fill in some of the gaps. I'm sure there are many more stories that could be written, but it is time to move forward.

Is this the end of Terry and Char? Hell no! The story of Terry and Char on Earth ends with Book 10, but there's a whole galaxy out there that needs to be explored. Nomad's Galaxy - an end and a beginning.

If you wonder about a character, don't hesitate to drop me a line. I have in my head what happened to them all. If you believe there is a positive outcome for certain characters, then it will be positive. Hope for a wonderful future is something that I believe in. If it's not turning out as you like, be like TH and shape your future with your own hands.

Control what is in your control.

With that, I'll leave you to it. Break's over for me, I need to get writing on The Bad Company before the boiling pepsi and pitchforks crowd appears in my driveway.

Peace, fellow humans.

———

Please join my Newsletter (www.craigmartelle.com – half way down the page – please, please, please sign up!), or you can follow me on Facebook since you'll get the same opportunity to pick up the books on that first day they are published.

If you liked this story, you might like some of my other books. You can join my mailing list by dropping by my website **www.craigmartelle.com** or if you have any comments, shoot me a note at craig@craigmartelle.com. I am always happy to hear from people who've read my work. I try to answer every email I receive.

If you liked the story, please write a short review for me on Amazon. I greatly appreciate any kind words, even one or two sentences go a long way. The number of reviews an ebook receives greatly improves how well an ebook does on Amazon.

Amazon – www.amazon.com/author/craigmartelle
Facebook – www.facebook.com/authorcraigmartelle
My web page – www.craigmartelle.com

Twitter – www.twitter.com/rick_banik

Thank you for reading the Terry Henry Walton Chronicles!

First THANK YOU for not only reading this book, but these author notes as well!

Right now in Florida, many of our collaborators (JIT / Fans / Operations / Collaborators) are either hunkering down for Hurricane Irma, or are leaving to a safer location. We wish you safety *always*!

I want to give a shout-out to Andrew Dobell for not only this cover, but DOZENS of covers that he has put together over the last year and a half working with myself, and then the collaborators on so many of these stories. He started with Death Becomes Her and then has worked not only on the Terry Henry Walton Chronicles, but those for Natalie Grey, Ell Leigh Clarke, and Sarah Noffke. Covers you will see soon include those for authors S.M. Boyce, JN Chaney, myself (Tabitha series), and Tom Dublin.

Hell, I might be missing a few, if so *sorry* Andrew!

If you are curious about Andrew's other covers and artwork - check him out here: http://www. creativeedgestudios.co.uk

Andrew also writes books (which is why I know about him, he was in the 20BooksTo50k group) and you can find his stories here: http://www.andrewdobellauthor.co.uk

This crazy story about Terry Henry Walton, Charamuti and the group around them is both ending, and beginning. Their time on Earth has come to a close, now they get to go and spread their metaphorical wings just a little more.

Once more, good friends, we go unto the breach.

Stand fast, good friends, as wave after wave strive to overtake us.

Go forward, good friends, looking evil in the eye and yell 'Eat this sword, feel the pain as we bring justice so painfully into your lives!'

Ok, so no (good) poet ever penned those words. But hell, I can imagine saying it.

;-)

Ad Aeternitatem,

Michael Anderle

Craig Martelle's other books (listed by series)

Terry Henry Walton Chronicles (co-written with Michael Anderle) – a post-apocalyptic paranormal adventure

Gateway to the Universe (co-written with Justin Sloan & Michael Anderle) – this book transitions the characters from the Terry Henry Walton Chronicles to The Bad Company

The Bad Company (co-written with Michael Anderle) – a military science fiction space opera

Judge, Jury, & Executioner (also available in audio) – a space opera adventure legal thriller

Shadow Vanguard – a Tom Dublin series

Superdreadnought (co-written with Tim Marquitz)– an AI military space opera

Metal Legion (co-written with Caleb Wachter) (coming in audio) – a military space opera

The Free Trader – a young adult science fiction action adventure

Cygnus Space Opera (also available in audio) – A young adult space opera (set in the Free Trader universe)

Darklanding (co-written with Scott Moon) (also available in audio) – a space western

Mystically Engineered (co-written with Valerie Emerson) – Mystics, dragons, & spaceships

End Times Alaska (also available in audio) – a Permuted Press publication – a post-apocalyptic survivalist adventure

Nightwalker (a Frank Roderus series) with Craig Martelle – A post-apocalyptic western adventure

End Days (co-written with E.E. Isherwood) (coming in audio) – a post-apocalyptic adventure

Successful Indie Author – a non-fiction series to help self-published authors

Metamorphosis Alpha – stories from the world's first science fiction RPG

The Expanding Universe – science fiction anthologies

Monster Case Files (co-written with Kathryn Hearst) – A Warner twins mystery adventure

Rick Banik (also available in audio) – Spy & terrorism action adventure

Published exclusively by Craig Martelle, Inc

The Dragon's Call by Angelique Anderson & Craig A. Price, Jr. – an epic fantasy quest

For a complete list of Craig's books, stop by his website – https://craigmartelle.com

BOOKS BY MICHAEL ANDERLE

For a complete list of books by Michael Anderle, please visit:

www.lmbpn.com/ma-books/

All LMBPN Audiobooks are Available at Audible.com and iTunes. For a complete list of audiobooks visit:

www.lmbpn.com/audible

CONNECT WITH THE AUTHORS

Craig Martelle Social

Website & Newsletter:
http://www.craigmartelle.com
BookBub:
https://www.bookbub.com/authors/craig-martelle

Facebook:
https://www.facebook.com/AuthorCraigMartelle/

Michael Anderle Social

Website:
www.lmbpn.com

Email List:
http://kurtherianbooks.com/email-list/

Facebook Here:
https://www.facebook.com/TheKurtherianGambitBooks/